The Day of the SCRAMBLED SIGNS

Written by Chris Callaghan

Illustrated by Amit Tayal

Collins

Shinoy and the Chaos Crew

When Shinoy downloads the Chaos Crew app on his phone, a glitch in the system gives him the power to summon his TV heroes into his world.

With the team on board, Shinoy can figure out what dastardly plans the red-eyed S.N.A.I.R., a Super Nasty Artificial Intelligent Robot, has come up with, and save the day.

Shinoy and Toby were taking turns playing Chaos Crew: Portals of Doom on Shinoy's phone.

"I'm always pressing the wrong button," Toby grumbled.

"You just need a bit more practice," said Shinoy. "You're doing really well."

His phone buzzed with a News Alert.

"Reports are coming in from Flat Hill about radioactive monsters on the loose and spaceships flying through the shopping centre!" read Shinoy.

Shinoy and Toby looked at each other in amazement.

"That must be from the Chaos Crew app or something," said Toby.

"No, it's the news. The real news!"

Shinoy switched on the TV and found the news channel. A serious-looking man with a serious-looking tie was talking.

"… from a shopping centre. Several reports of monsters and UFOs …"

Mum walked in and chuckled. "More fake news. Honestly, it's getting worse."

Suddenly, they heard cries and the sound of stamping feet outside. They all went to the window to look. Dozens of people ran down the street, shouting, "MONSTERS!"

Mum looked up into the sky and said, "Did they mention UFOs?"

"Call to Action, Chaos Crew!" Shinoy pressed the app on his phone.

A flash of light revealed warrior woman, Salama. She raced around the room making sure it was safe.

6

Bug appeared too. "Tech support, at your service. Any hot chocolate going?"

Shinoy explained what was going on, while Mum made a hot chocolate for everyone. She was a little annoyed when they all left without drinking it.

"Be careful of those monsters!" she called out.

"Don't worry," said Toby, turning back to grab a travel mug with hot chocolate in it. "I'll keep everyone safe."

Mum wasn't sure if she felt comfortable with that, so she decided to join them too.

More people were running down the street waving their arms around.

"They're coming from the shopping centre," said Shinoy. That made sense if all the monsters were there. He felt a tingle of excitement as they raced into danger. It felt great, and a little scary!

By the time they got to the shopping centre, it was completely deserted.

Bug was breathing heavily. "If I'd known there was going to be running, I'd have brought my Hyper Buggy. And my hot chocolate."

Toby handed her a travel mug. "I thought you might need this."

"You're a hero," she smiled.

They ducked down behind a wall.

Salama looked confused. "No evidence of monsters," she said, "and it does not feel like a High Gravity Area."

"What do you mean?" Shinoy asked. Salama pointed to the sign. It didn't make any sense, thought Shinoy. High Gravity Areas were common in the Chaos Crew world, but why should there be a sign like that here?

Shinoy saw another sign:

**Do Not Exceed
the Speed of Light**

And another:

**Warning:
Sonic Booms
in Operation!**

They'd replaced the normal signs like Toilets This
Way and Please Keep Off the Grass.
Even the advertising screens and logos above
the shops were different.

From up above, there was a thunderous noise. They couldn't see anything, but it was close. Maybe it was a UFO?

"Whaaaaaaaaaaaa!" A huge, brown, furry thing bounded through the shopping centre. Salama leaped into action and ran towards the monster.

Salama moved her shield in her trademark side-to-side swooshing pattern. It was used to confuse her enemy, and Shinoy watched, hypnotised. The monster seemed a little confused and not that scary, thought Shinoy.

Salama crashed into it and they went spinning into a floral display. Losing an arm in battle many years ago didn't stop the warrior grabbing a tight hold around the monster's neck.

Then its head fell off!

Everyone gasped. The head of a man popped up in its place, his face shocked.

"Are you an alien?" screamed the terrified man.

Salama was confused. "Are you a monster?"

The noise from above became louder and a voice boomed out,

"Has anyone seen any monsters or aliens?"

It was a police helicopter with a loudspeaker.

"I don't think there are any," shouted Shinoy, as they fought against the wind from the helicopter's blades. The helicopter drifted off on its monster hunt.

"The signs and notices are from the Chaos Crew world, but they don't fit in here." Shinoy pointed to the sign outside a coffee shop that read: Warning: Radioactive Monsters.

"Is he radioactive?" asked Toby, looking at the man in the fluffy costume.

"I hope not," the man gulped. "I've just opened up a new toyshop. I'm supposed to be Timmy the Teddy Bear."

Bug flipped down a screen from her headset and scanned the area.

"All the signs and words don't belong here," she said. "It's like some kind of setting change."

Toby gulped. "I changed the setting on the Portals of Doom game to Info Mode. A red pop-up message said it might help me with the controls."

"A *red* pop-up?" Shinoy immediately thought of the cunning S.N.A.I.R. He flicked through his phone and changed the game's options back to Gameplayer Mode. When he looked up again, all the signs, notices and words in the shopping centre had changed back to normal.

"There were never any monsters or aliens," said Shinoy, "just lots of people seeing strange signs, panicking and running away."

"Can you show me the setting for that?" asked Mum.

"Why?"

"Look how empty this place is. I could do my Saturday shopping in no time if it was like this!"

Fake news

Ideas for reading

Written by Clare Dowdall, PhD
Lecturer and Primary Literacy Consultant

Reading objectives

- discuss the sequence of events in books and how items of information are related
- make inferences on the basis of what is being said and done
- answer and ask questions
- predict what might happen on the basis of what has been read so far

Spoken language objectives

- give well-structured descriptions and explanations
- participate in discussions, presentations, performances and debates

Curriculum links: Art and Design – drawing and painting to share experiences and imagination; PSHE – Living in the wider world: that not all seen online is true

Word count: 965

Interest words: signs, UFO, rampaging, radioactive, fake news, warrior woman, trademark, notices

Resources: paper and pencils, whiteboards or notebooks, blank timelines or storyboards, digital cameras, ICT for research.

Build a context for reading

- Look at the front cover and read the title: *The Day of the Scrambled Signs.* Ask children what they think it means.
- Ask a volunteer to read the mission in the blurb. Check that children know what a UFO is, and what *rampaging* means.
- Using the front and back cover information, ask children to predict what might happen in Shinoy's adventure.

Understand and apply reading strategies

- Read p3 to the group. Pause reading to invite children to say how they would feel and what they would do if they received a News Alert at home about radioactive monsters and spaceships.